THE SEAL
OF GIJON

THE SEAL OF GIJON

OR, NICK CARTER'S ICE-HOUSE FIGHT

NICHOLAS CARTER

WILDSIDE PRESS

INTRODUCTION

Nick Carter is a fictional character who began as a dime-novel private detective in 1886 and has appeared in a variety of formats over more than a century. He first appeared in the story paper *New York Weekly* (Vol. 41 No. 46, September 18, 1886) in a 13-week serial, *The Old Detective's Pupil; or, The Mysterious Crime of Madison Square*.

The character was conceived by Ormond G. Smith, the son of one of the founders of Street & Smith, and realized by John R. Coryell. The character proved popular enough to headline its own magazine, *Nick Carter Weekly*. The serialized stories in *Nick Carter Weekly* were also reprinted as stand-alone titles under the New Magnet Library imprint.

By 1915, *Nick Carter Weekly* had ceased publication and Street & Smith had replaced it with *Detective Story Magazine*, which focused on a more varied cast of characters. There was a brief attempt at reviving Carter in 1924–27 in *Detective Story Magazine*, but it was not successful.

In the 1930s, due to the success of *The Shadow* and *Doc Savage*, Street & Smith revived Nick Carter in a pulp magazine (called *Nick Carter Detective Magazine*) that ran from 1933 to 1936. Since the Doc Savage character had basically been given Nick's background, Nick Carter was now recast as a hard-boiled detective. Novels featuring Carter continued to appear through the 1950s, by which time there was also a popular radio show, *Nick Carter, Master Detective,* which aired on the Mutual Broadcasting System network from 1943 to 1955.

The Seal of Gijon was originally published on April 24, 1915 in the nickel weekly *Nick Carter Stories* #137. It's part of a sequence of mystery stories that brought Nick and his associates to Joyalita, a small monarchy near the Caribbean Sea. The book has been lightly edited to modernize language and punctuation.

Enjoy!

—John Betancourt
Cabin John, Maryland

CHAPTER I

SLIPPED AWAY

"Look out! You'll run us down!"

The response was a growling oath, as the heavy launch came on, full speed, straight across the river.

Nick Carter, sitting at the wheel of another craft of the same type, saw the danger even before his assistant shouted this warning.

"Keep quiet, Chick!" he ordered, in his calm tones. "I'll make it!"

The famous detective had handled motor boats before, and he knew he could dodge the erratic craft cutting across his bows, unless the other man changed his course at the crucial moment.

They were abreast of Yonkers, and at that point the lordly Hudson is swift, as well as wide.

The launch coming across the river had suddenly appeared from the shadow of the Palisades, apparently bound straight for the busy city on the opposite shore.

In it were three men. The one at the wheel, who appeared to be in general command, had a square, bulldog sort of face, with heavy jaw, outstanding ears, and other features that make more for physical determination than beauty.

Another man, who scowled at Nick Carter and Chick with an evil intentness that made the latter long to jump on him and have it out there and then, sat in the stern and whispered something in the ear of the engineer. This second man was lean of face and evidently long of body. He had deep-set, unwinking eyes, and a square face at the bottom which suggested that he was at enmity with most of his kind.

With it all, there was a restless cunning in the far-buried eyes which made him even more unpleasant to contemplate than the man to whom he was whispering.

As if to counterbalance to some extent the preponderance of brutal humanity in the launch, the third passenger was a rather small, slight young man, who looked hardly old enough to vote. His face was pale and his eyes had a gentle, appealing expression, almost like that of a very innocent, unsophisticated girl.

Appearances are deceitful very often. So let it be stated at once that this gentle young fellow, barely out of his teens, and whose voice was as mild as his looks, was none other than Pet Carlin, one of the cruelest, most unscrupulous gangsters in New York City.

Carlin's name was supposed to be Peter. That had been shortened by his associates to "Pete." Afterward the final "e" had been clipped off, because of his inoffensive appearance and manner, and he was known as "Pet."

Nick Carter shut off his power, and manipulated the wheel carefully, as he saw that the man in the other boat was recklessly driving straight toward him.

There was only a narrow margin for the two launches to pass each other, but it would have been done successfully had not the stranger deliberately turned his wheel just as Nick Carter was gliding past in safety by the most skillful management of his helm.

"Larry!" exclaimed Pet, in a startled tone.

He was staring hard at the two passengers in Nick Carter's boat—two men who wore handcuffs on their wrists—and a quick look of recognition had passed back to him.

"What?" growled the man at the wheel, Larry Dugan. "What's biting yer, Pet?"

"Look!"

All three of the men in the launch gazed at the two handcuffed men, and all three expressed their astonishment in low grunts.

"Get 'em!" whispered the man behind the steersman—he of the deep-set, cunning eyes. "We've got to do it!"

It was just as this was said that the collision came.

The launch coming across the river headed straight for the middle of the other. Only because Nick Carter swung his wheel around, thus receiving a glancing blow, instead of one head-on, was his boat saved from being cut in two.

As it was, the two launches hung motionless for a moment, as two men might before they fell after receiving a mortal blow.

Then, as Nick gave another quick turn to his wheel, and at the same time opened the throttle, he slid past the other launch and was free, in the open water.

It was only for a moment, however.

The detective had seen, at the first glance, that the launch occupied by the three forbidding-looking men was superior to his own in the case with which it could be manipulated.

It was narrower in the beam, and the engine was more powerful. Besides, it answered to its helm more smoothly and promptly than his own.

Nevertheless, as Nick Carter, in that short instant, managed to get a full view of the faces of the men, he recognized them all. Also, he saw that they knew his two handcuffed passengers.

Further proof of this came at once, when, as Nick swung his launch clear, the man at the wheel of the other boat, with a snarl, twisted his wheel and again brought the two launches against each other, parallel, with a crash.

"Look out, Chick! Hold the gunwale of that other boat!" shouted Nick Carter. "Don't let them get away!"

"I should say not!" was Chick's response. "Don't you see who they are?"

"Of course I do!" shouted back Nick Carter. "That fellow at the wheel is Larry Dugan."

The detective had seen that three of the worst ruffians in New York—men who could be hired to beat, or even kill, a man, for pay—were in the launch, and he could not keep a horrible suspicion out of his mind which implicated Don Solado and Prince Miguel, his two handcuffed prisoners.

It was Nick Carter's determination now to catch the three thugs. He had little doubt that they had been hired by Solado and Miguel to make away with a man they wanted to keep out of sight, for a time at least.

The man's name was Prince Marcos.

In this supposition he was right. But he did not give the rascals credit for quite so much audacity as they possessed.

As Nick reached over the sides of the two launches which were rubbing against each other, and grabbed the man nearest to him, who happened to be Pet Carlin, there was a loud shout from Chick.

"Look out, chief! They're getting our men!"

The launches sprang violently apart, and Nick was obliged to let go of Pet to save himself from going overboard.

With his throttle wide open, sending the boat along at full speed, Nick swung around in pursuit of the other craft.

He had special reason to do this now, for, as Chick had warned him, the trio of ruffians had actually snatched away Don Solado and Prince Miguel, his handcuffed prisoners, under his very nose.

Only the fact that Nick had been hampered by his position at the wheel and the levers of the engine had enabled the rascals to be successful.

It was impossible for the detectives to move quickly—even if it had been safe to leave the launch to its own devices. He was obliged to keep his hand on the steering wheel, and to see that the engine was not running wild.

Larry Dugan, Foxey, and Pet all understood this, and they had taken instant advantage of the odds in their favor.

Pulling the two prisoners from one boat to the other, they had allowed them to lie down in the bottom, while Dugan, with a skill equal to Nick Carter's own, had sent his launch full speed toward the wharves and tangle of shipping that one always sees on the water front of Yonkers.

It was the multitude of craft of all kinds hiding the wharves that gave the three thugs their advantage.

Larry Dugan was unusually skillful in handling the launch, and he had a long start of Nick Carter before the latter could get his launch around, headed for shore.

It was broad daylight, but there was a bone-racking fog on the river, and it hid the escaping boat even as it plunged in among the anchored shipping and big lumber barges that stretched for a quarter of a mile, at least.

"They can't be far away," said Nick, as he pushed his launch along. "Keep a bright lookout, Chick!"

"All right!"

But the rascals knew this part of the river and the peculiarities of the water front of Yonkers as well as did Nick Carter, and they got clear away.

The fog helped them materially. They might never have dodged the pursuing boat otherwise.

The detective also knew Yonkers. But, because he did know it, he was quite aware that it would not be so very difficult for Larry Dugan to elude him, especially with the fog to help.

"They've beaten us, chief!" grumbled Chick, a quarter of an hour later. "They've gone along inside this line of barges and shot out at the end. While we have been poking about here, they've headed down the river."

"I think you're right, Chick," conceded Nick. "They'd hardly go up the river, of course. Well, we'll go down, too. We've lost our prisoners, but I don't care so much for that if they don't get hold of Prince Marcos."

"What is all this about Prince Marcos?" asked Chick. "I don't think I have ever got the story straight, in spite of all I've heard."

"It can be told in a few words," answered Nick. "Prince Marcos is the hereditary ruler of Joyalita, a small monarchy near the Caribbean Sea. He is a decent fellow, from all I've seen of him."

"Yes, I understand that," was Chick's quiet comment.

"Well, there is a party of grafters in Joyalita who would like the country, such as it is, to be annexed to another one adjoining. That would probably throw Prince Marcos out, and his Cousin Miguel who has just got away from us on that boat, would be made provisional ruler."

"I see. Miguel would get Marcos' job. But what is this about Marcos wanting to get home by the eighteenth?"

"If he gets to Joyalita on or before that date, he will be able to use his power to prevent the annexation."

"By a casting vote?" asked Chick.

"No. As head of the country and government, he won't have to vote. His word controls the situation."

"What they call a royal prerogative in Europe, eh?"

"Yes."

"And this other citizen in the handcuffs, Don Solado— where does he come in?"

"He is prime minister, and he is on the side of Miguel."

"It's all clear enough to me now," remarked Chick. "Don Solado and Miguel are trying to hold Marcos here till it will be too late for him to stop this big grafting annexation?"

"Exactly! We shall have to work like Trojans now to enable Marcos to win. I've pledged myself to do it, however, and we shall have to manage it, somehow," was Nick Carter's steady conclusion, as he turned the launch downstream. "We have Larry Dugan and his crowd against us, as well as Solado and Miguel. That will make it harder. But we can beat the gang if we stick to it."

"We'll stick to it, all right!" responded Chick, with that determined note in his voice which his chief knew meant business.

"That's what I like to hear, Chick. It won't be an easy task, but we have simply got to get Prince Marcos to Joyalita by the eighteenth of this month."

"You bet!" added Chick.

CHAPTER II

SECRET FOES AT WORK

In spite of the sharp lookout maintained by Nick Carter and his assistant for the launch with the five rascals in it all the way down to that upper part of Manhattan Island where New York City has reached only to give certain favored persons semirural homes, they saw nothing of the evil-faced Larry Dugan and his companions.

"There's Crownledge," pointed out Chick, as they came opposite the handsome house, in its own grounds, which Marcos and his mother had taken for a temporary residence.

The launch ran up to the landing, and Nick Carter, leaving his assistant to take care of the boat, went into the house.

He was met at the door by Claudia Solado, Marcos' cousin. The girl was delighted to see the detective.

"Mr. Carter, I am so glad you have come," she said, as she put her soft hand into his. "Marcos wants to start for Joyalita at once, and, really, he is not well enough. After all he passed through in escaping from Prince Miguel and my uncle, and being so nearly drowned, he is weak and feverish. I am sure that if he will stay in the house until to-morrow morning, he will be so much better that there will be no danger."

"You have not seen Don Solado, your uncle, or Prince Miguel, near Crownledge this morning, have you?" he asked.

"No. The last I saw of them was when you saved Marcos from drowning and allowed those two men to capture you to save him."

"That didn't hurt me much, you see," laughed Nick Carter. "They seemed to think they could hold me on that hired yacht of theirs up the river. But I got the better of them. If I had not, probably I should not be here now."

"Where are they?"

"I don't know. But so long as they are not bothering Marcos, I don't think we need care. Where is the prince?"

"In the library."

"May I see him?"

"Of course. He is anxious for you to go in. He saw you through the window, coming up from the river."

Marcos was a well-built, robust young man at ordinary times. But he did not look robust just now. His face was pale and his movements lacked their usual resiliency.

Notwithstanding all this, his resemblance to Nick Carter was startling. The features were alike, and even the poise of the head, the set of the shoulders, and the general attitude, were identical.

"This is a pleasure, Mr. Carter!"

As Prince Marcos said this, the girl actually looked closely at her cousin to make sure that he was speaking, and not the detective.

"Glad to see you are all right, sir," returned Carter. "You'll pardon my not calling you 'your highness,' will you not? In the first place, I do not think it would be wise for you to use your title while in New York, and then again I must confess it is much easier to me to speak as if you were an ordinary American or Englishman."

"Quite right, my dear Carter!" returned Marcos heartily. "I wish you would address me as plain Mr. Joyal. That will suggest my country to me, and the name does not smell of royalty, does it?"

He asked this with a naïveté that pleased the detective. There was no nonsense about Marcos.

"Very well, Mr. Joyal. That shall be your name hereafter. Where is your valet?"

"He is here. In the adjoining room. Phillips!"

As he called this name, Phillips came in, a tall, quiet-mannered young man in a plain business suit. He did not look like a valet. It was part of his latest instructions from his employer that he should not appear to be what he was. Marcos had wisely come to the conclusion that there must not be any suggestion of royalty about him or his entourage if he meant to get back in safety to his own realm within the time limit.

"You were hurt by those men who stole Prince Marcos—I mean, Mr. Joyal—from Crownledge, the night before last, were you not?" asked Nick Carter.

"Yes. But I am quite well now," answered Phillips composedly.

"I am glad to hear it. Mr. Joyal may need your help. He will be starting for Joyalita tonight."

"Very good, sir."

Phillips would have said "Very good!" if he had been told that he was to be led to execution that night, or if it had been decided to make him Prince of Joyalita. Which is by way of saying that he was a perfectly trained man-servant of the European type. Impassiveness was his trade-mark.

He withdrew now, without another word.

"My mother is at Newport, visiting friends, and desires to stay there for a month," remarked Marcos. "After that she will spend another month or two in this country. I am glad of it."

"So am I," said Nick Carter quietly. "It is better for the party that goes to Joyalita to be as small and unobtrusive as possible."

"Is it necessary to wait until tonight before Marcos goes?" asked Claudia. "Don't you think it will be dangerous for him to remain in New York all day?"

"I don't think so. But there would be some likelihood of the enemy spying out our doings in the daylight. We must get away without any brass-band accompaniment."

"Do you know where my Uncle Solado is now?" asked the girl.

"I do not," replied the detective.

This was the absolute truth. He did not know. He could have told how Solado and Miguel had been dragged away by Larry Dugan and his two fellow ruffians and carried off in a power launch. But that would only have led to more questioning, which he did not want.

"What time should we start?" asked Marcos.

"Not before nine o'clock," replied the detective decidedly. "It will be quite dark by that time, and we shall have a chance to slip away without being noticed."

"I suppose that is the better plan," assented Marcos. "It will seem like a long day, however."

"All the better," rejoined Nick. "You need a rest. These four hours may do you a world of good."

"You will not remain with me, I suppose?"

"I want to go down to my home to look after my mail and so on. But I will come back early in the afternoon."

"You have not had breakfast yet, have you?"

"I shall breakfast at home, with my assistant. And, by the way, he is waiting for me down by the river. Before I go, there is one thing I want to speak about. The other night, at the ball in the Hotel Supremacy, there came into my possession, in a curious way, a valuable jewel-incrusted watch, on which was the letter 'M' in diamonds, and—"

"Mr. Carter!" interrupted Marcos eagerly. "Have you that watch still? Can you get it?"

"The watch is in my safe. I intend to bring it to you today."

"Can you? Can you?" cried Marcos excitedly. "That watch means so much to me. It is more than a mere time-keeper or ornament. It is bound up in the destinies of the ruling house of Joyalita. I cannot tell you how important it is. The watch, with the fob attached, is known as the Seal of Gijon."

"The watch shall be restored to you when I come back this afternoon."

"You found it, you say?"

"At the Hotel Supremacy. It is claimed by Prince Miguel, your cousin," returned Nick Carter. "Mrs. van Raikes, who gave the ball at the hotel that night, enlisted my services to find the watch. I had it then, but I did not say so. I was sure that there was a significance attached to it which required that it should not be lightly passed along without my being sure that it did not get into improper hands."

"As a matter of fact, Mr. Carter, I may as well tell you that that watch is the insignia of the ruler of Joyalita. It has the character of the great seal used in most monarchies. I did not take it to the Hotel Supremacy that night. In fact, I never have been in the hotel at any time. It could have been taken there only by my cousin, Prince Miguel."

"How did he get it?"

"It disappeared from my desk, where I had it in a secret drawer."

"Who knew of that secret drawer besides yourself?"

"No one that I know of."

"Phillips?"

"Phillips is above suspicion," returned Marcos coldly.

"No doubt. But did he know of the secret drawer?" persisted Nick.

"He did not. I am sure of it."

"What other servants have had access to your room?"

"Only the maid who attended to the room, and she never was long enough there to get at the drawer. Phillips always makes it a point to go in and out of my apartment at short intervals when any one is there doing work of any kind."

"Hum!" was all Nick Carter replied to this. Adding: "Don't speak of what I have told you to anybody."

He went away, giving the assurance that he would return in the afternoon, and, after telling Chick to come home as soon as he had returned the boat to the man from whom it had been hired, Joe Travers, he hustled downtown as fast as a subway express could take him.

After breakfast and a change of clothing, Nick Carter's first action was to look in his safe to make sure that the jewel watch was safe.

He took it out and looked at it. When he had examined it for a few moments, he saw that there was a spring, evidently intended to be secret, hidden beneath the catch that opened the outer case.

"I should like to know what that spring controls," he muttered, as he looked at the watch under a strong light on his large library table. "But it is not my secret. If it has any bearing on the attack of Solado and Miguel upon Marcos, or if it was the principal inducement to Miguel to steal the article, I may learn something about it later. At all events, if there is anything more to interfere with the departure of Marcos from New York, I will keep this secret spring in mind."

The detective was accustomed to take clues wherever he found them, and it was his experience that trifles like this spring in the valuable watch often led to discoveries very much worth while.

He was still musing over the watch when his telephone bell rang.

Something seemed to tell him that there was a communication of importance trembling on the wire, and he responded with a sharp "Hello!"

"This is Claudia," was the response. "That you, Mr. Carter?"

"Yes. What is it, Miss Solado?"

"Your assistant, Mr. Chickering Carter—"

"Yes, yes?" cried the detective, as the girl paused.

"He has gone!"

"Gone? Where?"

"I can't tell you everything on the telephone," rejoined the girl. "But if you will hurry up to Crownledge, you will know what to do."

"I'll come right away," answered Nick. "But I wish you'd tell me where my assistant was when he disappeared."

"There was a scuffle in the house, and when Phillips and Jason went to see what it was all about, Mr. Chickering had gone. Please hurry!"

"I'll come at once, of course—be with you in about twenty minutes. But one more question. Who is Jason?"

"Phillips' assistant. The 'second man,' as they call him. He is a chauffeur in Joyalita, but has not acted in that capacity in New York."

"Mr. Marcos'—I mean Mr. Joyal's—servant, eh?"

"Yes. Under Phillips."

"I understand," replied Nick. "Good-by! I'll soon be with you."

"You will find me waiting for you," was the girl's agitated answer.

CHAPTER III

NICK CARTER TASTES SALT

When Nick Carter dashed up to the front entrance of Crownledge in his own big touring car, with Danny Maloney at the wheel, he found Claudia Solado on the porch, looking for him.

"Oh, Mr. Carter! I'm so glad you have come. He's gone!"

"Who? My assistant?"

"Marcos, my cousin."

"What do you mean? That there have been two disappearances?"

"Yes. Did they go together?"

"We don't know."

"Where was Marcos when he vanished?"

"The last seen of him was when he went into his bedroom to lie down for a nap. He is not strong, and Phillips advised him to take a sleep. He thought that a good idea, and Phillips went with him. My cousin leaned on his arm, and I noticed how pale and weak he seemed as he left the library, where he had been sitting."

"What does Phillips say about the disappearance? How long did he stay in the bedroom?"

"Only while my cousin lay down on the outside of the bed, with a quilt over him. Phillips put the quilt on, saw that he was comfortable, and that the electric-bell button, hanging loosely to a wire, was within reach of his hand on the pillow, so that he could call any one he might want without getting up. He told Jason to look in now and then, without disturbing my cousin."

"Who is this Jason? Was he born in Joyalita?"

"No. I think he came from New York about a year ago," replied the girl. "I am not sure. You know, English is the tongue generally spoken in Joyalita, although there is some little Spanish. Jason speaks English, but I fancy I detect a certain twang that you hear from many people in New York, especially those who were born there."

"We'll have Jason into the library and hear what he has to say," announced Nick, as he went into that room with Claudia.

"Jason has gone!"

It was the cool voice of Phillips. He had heard the conversation between Claudia and the detective, and had followed them into the library.

"Where's he gone?" demanded Nick Carter.

"I don't know, sir. I might say, if you please, that I have not been quite satisfied with Jason since we have been here," ventured Phillips.

"Why?"

"He has twice, to my knowledge, been away all night, without any one knowing it but me. He seemed very tired when he returned on both occasions. He told me he had been sitting up with a friend of his who was sick, and who lived downtown somewhere."

"Did you prove that to be untrue?" asked the detective.

"No, sir. But I took the liberty of examining his trunk one day when I had sent him on an errand that would keep him away for two hours. In the trunk I found two valuable watch movements—"

"Watch movements?"

"Yes, sir. The cases were not there. Just the movements. I was a watchmaker once, and I know the value of such things, although they are not easily disposed of, except to a watchmaker who might happen to want them."

"I understand," interrupted Nick. "What else did you find in his trunk? Anything suspicious?"

"Yes. There were two chisels, a pointed crowbar, or 'jimmy,' a pair of fine steel pliers, and an automatic revolver."

"I wonder whether they are in his trunk now?"

"No, sir. I have looked in it, and there is nothing but the ordinary clothing, and not much of that."

"He is in his regular livery, is he?"

"No, sir. He never wears that when he goes out on his private business. Even the trousers he changes, although there is nothing distinctive about them except a blue stripe down the outside of each leg, which would hardly be seen at night, anyhow."

"How did you open the trunk? Wasn't it locked?"

"No. And that is where I look upon Jason as a man of particular cunning," replied Phillips. "He must have found out that I had been examining his belongings—or suspected it. So he had shut down the trunk, without locking it, and put some of his clothes on top. That would enable him to see if I disturbed anything."

"Not if you put them back the same way," suggested Nick. "You could do that, couldn't you?"

"I tried. But Jason is a cunning rascal, I'm afraid, and he would be pretty sure to see that some one had been at his trunk."

"If you think he is dishonest, why do you keep him here? Mr. Joyal—the prince—would allow you to discharge him if you thought it well to do so, wouldn't he?"

"Yes. But I want to keep Jason till I can catch him in the act. Then I may find out several things that are distressing me. Mr.—er—Joyal has missed some valuable property, and we think Jason is the man who took it."

"What kind of property?"

Phillips looked from side to side, as if to make sure no one should overhear. Then he whispered:

"The Seal of Gijon is gone."

"I have heard of it," answered the detective. "It is a jeweled watch, with a diamond-mounted fob."

"That's it, sir," nodded Phillips. "The prince—I mean, Mr. Joyal—lost it several days ago. He is very anxious about it."

"Does he suspect Jason?"

"No, sir. There would have been no use in telling him that Jason was acting peculiarly until I had proof."

"What theory have you of the disappearance of Mr. Joyal?" asked the detective, changing the subject abruptly.

"None at all, sir. I can't account for it."

"Well, you keep a close watch around Crownledge. I may be back here this evening."

"I hope you will find Mr. Joyal."

"I will try," returned Nick, as he went out of the room, with Claudia by his side.

They walked to the front porch together. When Nick Carter had thrown a glance around, to make sure they were not followed, and that no one could overhear, he said to the girl, in a low tone:

"I wish you would stay at Crownledge for the remainder of the day, if you can. Keep a watchful eye on everything. It may be that Marcos has gone out for something that he thinks he should attend to promptly in his own person, and that my assistant has gone with him as a sort of bodyguard."

Claudia shook her head incredulously.

"I can hardly think that. My cousin would most likely have told me or Phillips, or both of us, if he had intended to be away even for half an hour. Besides, he was lying down when last seen by Phillips."

"Well, at all events, if you can stay here for the remainder of the day, it may help us materially. I still intend to leave here tonight with Marcos for Joyalita, if possible. If not, we will go not later than to-morrow."

"Do you know where Marcos is, then?"

"I know where he may be," answered Nick. "I am going to see."

His touring car was still at the front steps. With a smiling farewell and lifting of his hat to the girl, the detective took his place in the car and directed Maloney to take him home.

When Nick Carter told Claudia that he knew where Marcos might be, he was not speaking without reason. Nor was his guess so wild as to be almost uncertainty.

True, as he had come to his conclusion by a process of induction only. But it was a process that had served him well at every stage of his career, and he had the faith in it that is based on proven tests.

When he reached the porch of Crownledge with Claudia Solado, and glanced around him, his eye lighted on a trifle which his quick brain told him might not be such a trifle, after all.

Without the girl observing him, he stopped suddenly and picked up a small cake of mud and grass that evidently had dropped from somebody's shoe. From the shape of it, Nick knew that it had been wedged into the instep of a rather large shoe which must have belonged to a man.

The mass of soil, with half a dozen clipped-off blades of grass embedded in it, had filled all the space in the instep between the heel and the beginning of the sole.

When the detective picked it up, he held it carefully in the fingers of his left hand, so that it should preserve its shape until he was ready to examine it at his leisure. He held his hand at his side, and the girl took no notice of it.

Until the car reached Madison Avenue, and he had told Danny Maloney, the chauffeur, that he might want him again at night, but that he need not stay any longer then, Nick Carter contented himself with surveying his prize casually as it lay flat on the palm of his hand.

No sooner was he locked in his library, however, than he closed the blinds, and, having lighted a cigar, turned his strong incandescent light down upon his table.

On a sheet of white paper he laid the mass of mud and grass.

It was nearly dry. Therefore, it was possible to handle it without its losing its shape.

"I don't think I can be mistaken," muttered Nick. "I think I know this wiry grass too well, and this sandy mud is of a kind that is not found in many places hereabouts. However, I'll look at it through my glass."

He took a very strong magnifying glass from his table drawer and studied the mixture for nearly half a minute.

As he put the glass down, a satisfied smile flickered across his strong face.

"There is just one more test," he muttered. "Although I believe it is superfluous. However, here goes."

He put the tuft of grass to his tongue.

"I knew it," was his soft exclamation. "Salt! It could not be anything else."

He pressed a push button at the side of his table, and then unfastened the door of the room. As he returned to his seat, he puffed contentedly at his cigar, still regarding the mud and tuft of grass on the white paper.

"Want me, chief?"

A young fellow, with the bright, alert expression on his rather thin features that tells of an active brain, stood in the doorway.

"Yes, Patsy! Close the door and come over here."

The young man obeyed, and Nick Carter pointed to the stuff on the paper on his table.

"What's that, Patsy?"

Patsy Garvan—for it was the trusted young assistant of that name who had come in—bent closely over the paper and studied the grass for a moment.

"I should say it is salt meadow grass," he answered.

"Why do you think so?"

"It is coarse, and there is a color to it you don't see in any other kind. If you'll let me taste it, I can tell you."

Nick Carter laughed and drew several whiffs of smoke from his cigar before he spoke again.

"That's just what I did, Patsy," he said, at last. "Put your tongue to it and let me know what you think."

Patsy lifted the paper and put out his tongue.

"I should say so," was his remark, as he replaced the paper and its contents on the table. "Gee! You couldn't fool me on that. Where did you get it?"

"Never mind about that, Patsy. Where do you suppose this grass and mud came from?"

"Hackensack meadows, of course! Have you been over there?"

"No. But the man from whose shoe this came must have been. Look here Patsy! Chick has been taken away against his will—"

"What?" blurted out Patsy Garvan. "Chick? Say! Let me—"

"And one of the men who took him dropped this mud and grass from his shoe."

"He did? Say, chief! We're going after Chick right away, ain't we?"

Patsy was on his feet, his fists clenched, and anger blazing all over his face.

He had a regard for Chick only second to that he felt for Nick Carter himself. The thought of his chum being held anywhere made him frantic.

"Keep cool, Patsy! We'll go, of course! But we'll have to be careful."

"How do you mean careful?"

"This is the open season for duck hunting, and there are any number of ducks over there, in the meadows."

"Sure! But I don't quite get you? What do I care for the darned ducks?"

"Put on that leather coat you have," directed Nick calmly. "And your high boots, as well as your big corduroy cap. Get your double-barreled gun and that string of wooden decoy ducks we used down on the Chesapeake two years ago. You have them, haven't you?"

"Yes."

"Very well. Don't be more than ten minutes. Then come down to the library again. I'm going to put on my duck-hunting rig, too."

CHAPTER IV

THE ICE HOUSE IN THE SWAMP

It was hardly ten minutes later when Patsy came again into the library. But, rapid as he had been in his movements, he had not been able to beat his chief.

Nick Carter was already in the room, dressed in about the same kind of clothes as he had told his assistant to put on. That is, he wore a heavy leather coat, with pockets of various sizes all over it, a cap that hid most of his face, and rubber boots which came up to his hips.

He carried a handsome repeating shotgun—light, but deadly, in the hands of a sure shot like the detective.

Glancing at himself in a mirror, Nick was satisfied that he would not be easily recognized. To make sure, he put on a heavy beard and mustache, with the result that he did not look any more like the real Nick Carter, than he did like Mrs. Pankhurst.

"Keep your cap well down, Patsy," he directed. "Your face is not well known to these people we are going after. But some of them may have seen you."

"What's the plan of campaign?" asked Patsy, as they crossed in a ferryboat to Hoboken.

"That will develop as we go on," replied Nick. "Here's a street car that will take us across the meadows—or as far as we want to go."

The Hackensack meadows cover a very wide expanse in New Jersey, a little way back from the bay and Hudson

River. They are called "meadows." Really, they are marshes over most of their extent, and duck shooting and fishing are the uses most people make of them.

There are solid spreads of ground here and there, and several lines of railroad cross and recross them.

As a rule, however, the meadows are decidedly sloppy, and as the water that floods them comes from the sea, everything is salt about them. The grass cut from these meadows is used mainly for bedding for cattle. As fodder it is useless.

It was at a dreary, desolate spot in the middle of the marshes that Nick Carter got off the car, with Patsy Garvan, and waited in the road as the car went spinning away farther into the back country.

"We'll get a boat here, Patsy," said Nick.

This was soon arranged. There was a boathouse close by, and from it any one could hire a flat-bottomed rowboat, warranted not to capsize easily, in which the occupant could penetrate the high grass, and thus lie in wait for ducks as long as suited him.

He could fish, too, if he liked. There is a great deal of fish in the waters of the meadows, and it is a favorite resort for anglers, as well as duck hunters.

It was a dull day, and there was a heavy fog. But that was not enough to discourage an enthusiastic duck hunter, as Nick remarked to the boat owner before they started.

He did not tell that smiling individual that fog was just what he wanted, although, if he had, he would have been telling the exact truth.

"Do you see that barn over there, Patsy?" he asked, when they were well among the reeds and rushes. "It's a big one, over to the right."

"An ice house, isn't it?" was Patsy's response.

"It was at one time, but it hasn't been used for that purpose lately. Do you see some smoke coming from the chimney at this end?"

"By jing! I do! Is there somebody living in there!"

"I should say so, if there is a fire in the place. If I am not much mistaken, we shall find certain gentlemen in that building who know me. They may know you, too. That I am not so sure about."

"Do you mean that you think Chick is in there?" asked Patsy, who had been turning things over in his mind. "Is that the idea?"

"I don't know about that. But I do think there may be somebody in the place that I want to find. Of course, I want to find Chick. But I do not fear that he is in trouble. The person I am after is called Prince Marcos—"

"What? Is it that Marcos case we're on?" broke in Patsy. "I thought he'd gone back to his own country, wherever it is. You said so a few days ago. At least, you said he was going."

"That was a week ago," Nick Carter reminded him. "Before I had anything to do with the case. Now I know better. He is in New York, somewhere, and I have to find him."

"I wish I knew a little more about the case," grumbled Patsy. "That would make it easier for me to work."

"I don't know that it would make it any easier," was Nick Carter's dry rejoinder. "You know that all I require of you as a rule is to obey orders—unless you are on a case by yourself."

"That's so," rejoined Patsy, with a sly grin. "But I've heard you say that no rule should be so iron bound that it cannot be twisted when the occasion calls for it. All I would like to know, if you see fit to tell me, is what we are after."

Patsy Garvan was not sure in what way his chief would receive this rebellious protest. He was relieved, therefore, when he saw Nick smile.

"I'll tell you that much," conceded the detective: "There is a man called Miguel and another named Solado who are trying to prevent Prince Marcos getting back to his own country by the eighteenth. I believe they are holding Marcos in this old ice house."

"And what about Chick?" asked Patsy.

"I don't know."

"Do you think he is in this place, too?"

"He may be. We are going to find out."

"That's the talk," responded Patsy. "Let's hurry! How are you going to get in? Knock at the front door?"

"Hardly!" said Nick. "You see that window at the top of the building? It is a door, in fact, boarded up."

"Yes."

"And you see the chute from it to the water? That is where they used to draw up the ice when it was brought here in boats. They did not get ice from these salt meadows, of course. But there are fresh-water streams not far away, and the ice was brought from them and stored here, handy to send to Jersey City and Hoboken."

"Well?" asked Patsy.

"I am going up that chute."

"You'll be seen, won't you?"

"Not likely. In the first place, there is a heavy fog, and, secondly, the windows in the living portion of the building are on the other side."

"You seem to know a great deal about this old ice house," observed Patsy.

"I do. This is not the first time I've looked it over. I should have made an investigation here soon, even if there had been no Prince Marcos case."

Patsy Garvan would have liked to ask why. But he felt that he had catechized his chief about as much as was safe. So he held back his curiosity and prepared to obey orders.

"Row the boat right up to that chute, Patsy."

"All right! But it doesn't reach down to the water."

"I see that. It does not matter. I can reach the bottom of it when I stand up in the boat."

Watched by the wondering Patsy, Nick Carter waited till the flat-bottomed boat had run directly under the end of the chute. Then he caught the chute and tested its strength as well as he could while standing in the wabbly little craft.

The chute was supported by strong iron rods that extended from the wooden wall, keeping it at the proper angle, so that it was easy to slide the blocks of ice upward by means of a block and tackle.

As Nick Carter had said, the building was capacious enough to accommodate many tons of ice, and it had been used as a storehouse for a long time.

Of later years, when facilities for handling ice were better, and when large corporations controlled the industry, there was no room for this small concern to continue in business.

So they had sold out, and the storehouse had been empty for years until within the past few months.

So, when a tenant offered himself, the owner of the building—who had almost forgotten that it was in existence—was only too glad to accept a nominal rental.

Who the tenant was Nick Carter had found out within the last twenty-four hours, and for that reason when he discovered the cake of mud, with salt grass embedded in it, he had not much doubt that he would be able to find Prince Marcos if he followed this clue.

"What are you going to do?" asked Patsy.

"That will depend on what I find when I get to the top of the chute. Keep the boat well hidden in the rushes as soon as I am out of it."

Patsy nodded. Then he gave his chief a hoist to help him into the bottom of the chute, and watched admiringly to see Nick Carter making his way up the treacherous runway, partly on the tips of his toes and partly on hands and knees.

At the top was a closed door. The fastening was not difficult, and as Patsy backed his boat into a thicket of long grass, he saw Nick Carter open the door and go in.

For ten minutes Patsy watched the door, but no one came out, and there was no sound from within.

"I'll wait here a little while. Then I'll go in after him," declared Patsy to himself.

CHAPTER V

COLD-BLOODED PLOTTING

When Nick Carter entered the building he found himself in a large, half-dark warehouse that had formerly held many tons of ice.

A great quantity of moldy sawdust was scattered about, and the thick boards of the flooring were broken in many places.

In one corner of the great room was a small trapdoor. Nick lifted it and found that a straight ladder led to another warehouse, not so lofty as the one above. Evidently it had been used to store ice, too.

The detective could not understand why there should be this separate storeroom until he had examined a long tank at one end, and found that it was an ammonia generator, with an engine underneath.

"They used to make artificial ice here, I see," muttered Nick Carter.

He walked very softly across the floor, because he was convinced that in the room below there were persons who would come after him quickly if they were aware of his presence.

In a corner of this second room was a sort of vestibule, with two doors.

It was easy to open these doors, for neither was locked.

The detective found himself at the top of a long flight of stairs which turned sharply not far from the bottom.

From where he stood he could look down into what appeared to be an office, furnished with a roll-top desk and a chair.

There was other furniture, no doubt. But the desk and chair were all Nick could see, except the old linoleum with which the floor was covered.

Low voices came to him—so low that if his ears had not been sharper than those of most people, he would not have been able to make out what was being said.

As it was, he not only caught the words, but also he recognized the voices as those of Don Solado and Prince Miguel.

Solado was speaking when Nick Carter first heard any of the conversation, and what he said was of personal interest to the detective.

"Now we know who that man is who pretended to be Marcos," were Solado's words, bitten off with a spitefulness that told how viciously in earnest he was, "the thing to do is to get him out of the way."

"Permanently?" asked Miguel, in a languid tone.

"Permanently," came the quick assent. "We can't afford to have an interfering individual like him disturbing us when we are planning for the welfare of our beloved country, Joyalita."

"Solado!" interrupted Miguel.

"Well?"

"You would oblige me if you were not quite so much of a humbug."

"Your highness?" spluttered Solado, his tone indicating that he was much scandalized.

"You know what I mean, Solado," was the imperturbable response. "Don't be so confoundedly diplomatic. Call a spade a spade, and don't try to fool either yourself or me."

"I don't understand—"

"Oh, yes, you do. This talk about working for the welfare of our beloved country is all very well when you are speaking for the benefit of strangers, and I have no objection to your giving it to Marcos, himself. But it only wastes precious time when you and I are alone together."

Nick Carter listened with more intentness than ever. He had learned, at the very beginning, that there was a plot to kill him—or to get him out of the way for a long time. He did not quite know what was meant by "permanently," although he could guess. But he had found out now that Marcos was somewhere close at hand—doubtless in the power of these two traitorous rascals.

"What I was going to say," went on Solado, "is that there is a strong reason for getting this American detective out of the way. He is taking too active a part in this matter. I do not feel that we have Marcos safe even now until we have pared the claws of Carter."

"You're right to a certain extent, Solado," was the response. "It would be well to stop this detective if we could. But I suggest that our first business is to take Marcos away, so that there will be no danger of his getting back to Joyalita by the eighteenth."

"Isn't he safe enough here?" asked Solado.

"He would be safer out at sea. Then we should not have to fear the detective, even though we were not able to dispose of him—permanently, as you so humanely put it," returned Miguel, with a grin.

"The blackguards!" muttered Nick Carter, over their heads.

"You forget that assistant of his," came from Solado, in response to Miguel's suggestion. "What are we to do with him?"

"I thought it was settled what was to be done with him," answered Miguel, in a more earnest tone than he yet had used. "There is a lot of ammonia stored in the lower part of this building. isn't there?"

"Yes, but—"

"There is no 'but' about it," broke in the other man impatiently. "If you only had a little more red blood in you, Solado, instead of being always afraid to do what common sense dictates, we should have had Marcos safe long ago, and we shouldn't be bothered with this detective and his man, as we are. Are you going to forget that he had handcuffs on us, and that, if it hadn't been for Dugan and his men, we might have been in that prison over in New York now?"

"I haven't forgotten anything," hissed Solado. "There will be an international inquiry into that outrage when we get back to Joyalita. The heir presumptive to the throne and the prime minister can't be treated as felons without making trouble."

"Bah!"

"I mean what I say!" shouted Solado, who seemed to lose control of himself as he thought of the indignity that had been put upon him. "We are guests of a civilized country—men of substance and wealth. We were torn away from our private yacht and treated like criminals, just because this man, Nicholas Carter, seems to be in the way of Prince Marcos."

"A good way to put it," sneered Miguel. "And I have no objection to your taking up the matter with the United States government when once we are safely in our own country. At present, it would be well to take the law into our own hands."

"What do you mean?"

Miguel leaned a little closer to his fellow conspirator, so that the light of the kerosene lamp fell full upon the hard, evil features of the pair. Nick Carter instinctively bent over the crazy banister to listen.

"I mean just this, Solado: If this place should accidentally catch fire, there is ammonia enough stored in the basement to make a smoke that would soon settle the business of any one who had to inhale it—"

"Well?"

"Where is that fellow?"

"Who? The assistant? He's down there somewhere. So is Marcos."

"They're not together?"

"Of course not. Dugan put them in separate cellars. There are four cellars and they have been used as storage places for different materials ever since the building was no longer used as an ice house."

"You have allowed Marcos to have cigarettes?"

"Yes. He smokes most of the time. That's his chief amusement—except when I go down to see him. Then he changes his occupation by abusing me."

"Very well. Where are Dugan and his men?"

"They are coming tonight to help me get Marcos away. It isn't safe to leave him here. The house stands by itself, and we don't know who might come to see what we are doing."

"Dugan has it leased at present, hasn't he?"

"Yes. He has some portable property he did not want to keep in New York, so he took this place for a year, under the name of Morrison. And there is a lot of stuff in one of the four cellars belonging to him. He will take that tonight, when we move Marcos. His men will be with him, and he will do everything at once."

"Where did you intend to put Marcos?"

"Dugan has a place where he will be safe—in New York. It is a tenement somewhere. He would not give me the address, but he will take us all there."

"I think the yacht would be the best plan. Let it go away, down the coast somewhere. Then perhaps we could lose Marcos in Mexico. You know there is a lot of promiscuous shooting in that region at present. It would need only a bare hint to make some of those officious Mexicans take a man as a spy and shoot him before he could explain."

Miguel was a savage-looking fellow at best. When he made this deliberately cold-blooded proposition he looked positively fiendish.

"Very well," returned Solado. "I'm willing. But we will leave the other fellow in the cellar."

"You mean Carter's man?"

"Yes."

For a few seconds the two plotters looked directly into each other's eyes. Then, slowly, each reached a hand across the table, and the two shook hands upon it.

"The scoundrels!" muttered Nick Carter. "I'm glad I got here in time. Actually they are going to kill Chick right in this building. They can't mean anything else. Well, I'll—"

He turned quickly, determined to get out, go down the chute, and, with Patsy, make his way to the basement in another way.

It would not be difficult to effect an entrance, for all the doors were of old and weather-rotted wood, and he could break through any of them, he was sure.

When once he had Chick and Marcos outside in safety, he would go after Solado and Miguel. He was resolved, too, that they would not get away this time.

Later, he would lay a trap for Dugan and his gang, and thus clean up the whole job in a neat and expeditious way, and without the expenditure of very much labor.

Probably Nick Carter would have carried out his plans exactly as he had planned them, but for an unforeseen accident.

As he turned to go away from the place where he had been standing on the stairs, listening to the edifying conversation below, he chanced to lean rather hard against the banister.

With a loud crack, it gave way. The detective, losing his balance, turned a complete somersault to the room below, landing on his head and shoulders on the table.

The table collapsed under his weight; the lamp smashed—fortunately, going out, instead of blowing up—and Nick Carter, stunned, and for the moment helpless, felt himself rudely grasped by somebody and tumbled in a heap down a steep flight of stairs.

When he reached the bottom he was quite unconscious.

CHAPTER VI

HOW PATSY BROKE IN

The blow on the head, suffered by the detective when he fell to the table, had been a severe one, and, aggravated by another tumble when the table crumpled up beneath him, it had inflicted worse injuries than might have been thought by any one who had seen the catastrophe.

It was hours before Nick Carter came to himself. When he did, he was in pitch-darkness, and he realized, from the peculiar, damp smell, that he was in a cellar.

Also, he caught a pungent odor, which he recognized, and which reminded him of the conversation he had heard just before he plunged through the broken banister.

"Ammonia, as sure as I am here," he muttered. "I'll have to move quickly, for it seems to me as if the stuff has been disturbed lately. If it has, probably it means—"

The thump of an engine made him pause.

"The fiends! They are generating the ammonia gas, and, of course, they will set it free by opening some of the valves, and then—"

The smell of ammonia waxed stronger, and his breath began to come with difficulty.

He fumbled along the rough stone wall, damp with the ooze of the marsh, until he came to an iron tank, from which the fumes were emerging so strongly that he reeled away, half suffocated.

"This won't do. They'll get me like a stray dog in a gas chamber if I don't find my way out."

The thumping of the engine continued, and his sense of direction told him that it was against the wall in which was a heavy door.

"There is a pump and it works underneath the tank in some way," muttered Nick. "I can't get at it on this side. The only chance would be to get to the other room, and the door is too heavy to be broken down in a hurry. I have no tools, and—"

"Gee! That's a bum smell!"

It was Patsy Garvan's voice, almost at his ear.

"Patsy!" he cried.

"Chief! Where are you?"

"In the cellar. Get in, quickly!"

"Hold on a moment!" came back the answer. "This is all fast water out here. I'm in the boat. Wait till I find the window."

Nick Carter understood now that the front of the building was in the water and high grass, while at the back it looked upon a rushing stream.

He made a short survey of his quarters.

"I see some boards that look as if they are nailed on at one place on the wall. I can't reach them, but I dare say you can kick them open. Try, at all events," he directed.

"All right! Gee! This is a stunt for an orphan boy. It has me going, I'm telling you. Holy mackerel! If this boat would only behave a little. It's swinging around like a skidding auto. I wish I'd put the chains on! Wow! There she goes!"

Patsy Garvan was uttering all these ejaculations in low tones, but they were none the less earnest on that account.

He had waited for what he considered a long enough time, and then had just been preparing to go up the chute, when he heard the crash as Nick Carter went through the banisters.

"Gee! Something's broke loose!" exclaimed Patsy then. "Me for the high grass!"

He had dropped back into the boat and shot away into the tangle of rushes.

Nobody had appeared at the front of the building, and he could not see the back. So he kept in hiding for half an hour or so, and then ventured up the chute once more.

This time he crawled to the very top. But the rascals within had investigated to find out how Nick had got in, and when they found the door at the top of the chute a little way open, they had carefully bolted it within.

It required only this bolted door to assure Patsy that some trick had been played on his beloved chief, and he cautiously made his way around the large wooden building.

He noted that there was a strong stone wall foundation, and when he saw that there were three square openings, each secured by heavy boards within, he understood that a large and water-tight cellar was part of the equipment of the warehouse.

When he heard Nick Carter tell him to kick in the boards at one of the windows it was perfectly clear to him what he was to do.

Holding his boat firmly at the boarded window where he had first caught the fumes of ammonia, and which had called forth his ejaculation, he warned Nick by saying cautiously:

"Chief!"

"Well?"

"Look out! I'm going to stave in this board with the end of the boat. It may hurt you if you get in the way."

"The boat is below the level of the window, isn't it?" asked Nick.

"Just a little," was Patsy's reply. "If it wasn't, the water would pour into the cellar."

"Then, how are you going to get the end of the boat against the boards, Patsy?"

"I'll tilt the end, and bring it up against the window with the bow for a battering-ram. Get me?"

Nick smiled in the darkness at the ingenuity of his assistant, but he merely told Patsy to go ahead, without any more comment.

There was a pause, as Patsy rowed his boat a few yards from the wall.

He had quite worked out in his own mind how he meant to force his way.

The boat was heavy and flat-bottomed. Any extra weight at one end would always cause the other to stand up clear of the water.

The wall of stone that formed the foundation of the big wooden building was only a few inches above the level of the still water.

It was safe to have it thus, because there were no tides, no disturbances of the surface at any time, or, at least, very few.

The tall reeds and grass made such a protection that the water was practically stagnant most of the time.

Patsy made his way to the stern, and also carried there the oars, a can of bait, a landing net, boat hook, and other things in the boat, as well as the two guns belonging to himself and Nick Carter.

"I'll weight it down all I can," he said to himself.

The bow of the boat shot up in the air so that it would easily clear the top of the stone foundation. It was pointing directly at the boards Patsy was prepared to attack.

The water was not deep at this point—in fact, at one time, there had been ground, more or less solid, above the surface—so Patsy dug the end of an oar into the bottom and, with a hard shove, sent the boat full tilt against the boards.

There was a crash as the end of the boat tore its way through. At the same time the fumes of ammonia gushed forth so fiercely that they tainted all the outside atmosphere.

Patsy was hurled flat upon his back, and the oar broke in two and floated slowly away.

The bow of the boat remained on the edge of the stone wall, poking a little way into the cellar.

"Chief!" cried Patsy. "Are you there?"

"Of course I am," was the reply. "Can't you get that boat out of the way, so that I can crawl out?"

"Sure! Just hold your mules a minute! She's in pretty tight—as the butcher said to the pound of sausage meat—but I can pry her out, I guess. In fact, I have to. Gee! She went in for keeps, but her little cousin, Patsy, wants her outside!"

Chattering thus, hardly knowing what he said, Patsy stood in the bow and shoved against the wall with all his strength.

The result was what he might have expected, although, perhaps, he had not thought of it. The boat slipped away from him, and he found himself clinging to the stone wall, his head in the cellar—where the fumes of ammonia made him cough—and a large expanse of empty water under his legs and feet.

"Holy Samuel!" he gasped. "Here's more of it!"

He got to one side of the ledge, so that Nick Carter had room to crawl out, and looked in dismay at the boat slowly drifting away.

"There's only one thing to be done, Patsy!" observed Nick.

"I know it. But I ain't going to get wetter than I'm obliged," was Patsy's prompt response. "I'll leave my duds behind me."

The opening of the window had allowed so much of the ammonia to escape that it was possible to remain on the ledge without suffering very much. So Patsy dropped inside the cellar, with his face to the air, and divested himself of his garments.

"I'll bring the boat back in a jiffy!" he announced. "Stay here till I get back, chief!"

With much cheerfulness, Patsy let himself down into the water, and swam over to the boat. Then he climbed in and rowed back to the window.

While Nick Carter got in, his good-tempered young assistant retrieved his clothing, and in a few minutes was dressed again.

"That's better than getting everything soaked with water!" observed Patsy. "It didn't take long, and it wasn't any worse than going in swimming with the boys the way I used to do."

"I'm glad I'm out of that place, Patsy!" said Nick Carter, with a smile of gratitude. "But we've still got to get after Chick and Prince Marcos."

"You bet!" agreed Patsy earnestly. "Think they are in this place somewhere?"

"You haven't seen anybody come out, have you?"

"No. I'll take my solemn oatmeal nobody came out while you were inside. I've been going around this shanty steadily."

"Then the gang must be inside still," declared Nick Carter. "My belief is that they have some other office room beside the one I saw them in, and that they are there now."

Patsy looked at his chief with a puzzled expression. Nick Carter had not told him anything about his adventures in the warehouse, and he did not understand in the least how Nick had come into the cellar.

Patsy Garvan could guess, though. He was as skillful at putting two and two together and getting at the result, as anybody in Nick Carter's circle of acquaintance—and that is saying a great deal.

"How many are there in the gang?" asked Patsy.

"Only two, that I know of for certain. But I am inclined to think there must be some more. Larry Dugan—"

"What?" broke in Patsy. "Is that murdering skunk in it?"

"I believe so," returned Nick seriously. "But I don't believe he is in this house at present."

"You don't? Why?"

"Because I heard the people inside say that he was coming at dark, to take Marcos away."

Patsy turned quickly to his chief, his face twitching with anxiety.

"And Chick? He's the boy I'm interested in. Dear old Chick!"

"That's right. We have to look after Chick," was Nick Carter's response.

Patsy Garvan involuntarily pulled back his coat cuffs, as if getting ready for action.

"Let's get busy!" he said. "If Chick's in this place, we're going to have him out. And if Larry Dugan and his crowd are coming tonight, we have no time to lose. It's getting dark now."

"We'll row around to that back door, Patsy," was the quiet way Nick Carter issued his order.

CHAPTER VII

CHICK'S FELLOW PRISONER

We must go back to the early morning, at Crownledge, to find out how Marcos and Chick had been kidnapped in the very midst of their friends.

The only thing Chick knew was that, when he had taken the power boat back to its owner, Joe Travers, he was coming up through the grounds of the big residence, and suddenly found himself overpowered by several men whom he could not see.

A sandbag knocked him nearly senseless, and then a bag was pulled over his head and he was carried some little distance, until he felt himself in a boat, rocking rather violently.

He soon recovered entire consciousness, but found his arms bound so tightly outside the sack that he could not move.

There was rather a long trip on the boat, which, from its sound and motion, he soon knew to be a power launch, and then he was made to step ashore and walk up a hill.

A ride in a motor car, followed by a short trip in a rowboat, was Chick's experience. He was thrown into some chamber, the dampness of which penetrated the sack and his other clothing, and sent a chill through him. Before he was left alone the ropes were taken from his arms.

He heard a door slam while struggling to get the sack off his head and shoulders.

When he did release himself, he did not find that he could see much better, although some chinks of light showed here and there and convinced him that he was in a cellar.

It must be remembered that Chick had not seen the outside world during any part of his captivity. The sack was a thick one. Moreover, he had been in a horizontal position in both boats.

Even in the automobile he had been compelled to lie in the bottom, with his shoulders resting against the seat.

The fact that he had a great deal of room in the car told him that it was a large one. But that was not much to go by. There are many makes of large cars which seem to be identical when one has no chance to look them over.

Chick noticed that this one rode very easily. Hence he had reason to suppose it was of an expensive type. Aside from that, he could not have distinguished it from any of half a dozen high-priced motor cars with which he was familiar.

"Well, this is cheerful!" thought Chick, as he moved about his cellar and discovered that there was nothing in it but a heap of sawdust and a very moldy smell. "Sawdust, eh? That looks as if it might be an ice house. Let me put on my considering cap, and see whether I can figure this thing out. I ought to be able to do that, even if I have been sandbagged."

He let his thoughts travel back to the moment when he was stricken down in the grounds of Crownledge, and then, bit by bit, put the evidence together until he had pieced it out to the present time.

"Let me see!" he murmured. "We had a short ride on a rather rough sea to begin with. There were the short, choppy waves of the Hudson, and they got a little longer after a while. Then they shortened up again. Good!"

He did not speak for a few moments, as he digested this, and sought for an explanation.

"I have it! They took me down the river a little. Then they crossed. The choppy waves are at the sides of the river, and the long ones in the middle. That's how I know they took me across. Yes, by George! There's another thing! We got in the way of a ferryboat and might have been run down. I'd forgotten that."

How Chick became aware of that incident, with a bag tied over his head and shoulders, lying in the bottom of the boat, can be logically explained.

He had heard the screeching of the ferryboat's siren, responded to by the toot of the power boat. Then there had been a great deal of hoarse language—profane, probably—followed by a jolting of the motor boat as it was swung around so sharply that it might have upset, followed by comparative quiet and the steady coughing of the motor as they went along.

"If we hadn't been in the middle of the river we should not have been likely to get in the way of a ferry," was the way Chick figured it out. "Well, that means that we came over to Hoboken, or somewhere along the Jersey side of the river, where a small boat could land. Of course! I get it now! It's all an open book!"

He slapped one hand on his knee and actually grinned. He was in a bad fix, and he knew it. But the thought that he had unraveled a problem, perhaps as well as it could have been done by Nick Carter himself, gave him such satisfaction that, for the moment, he cared for nothing else.

"I was yanked out of the boat and put in a motor car," he continued half audibly. "Very well! Before I got into the automobile I had to climb up a hill. That makes it all the more binding. I know the roads at the top of the hill, and I would bet a hundred dollars that I'm in the Hackensack meadows somewhere."

A few minutes more of cogitation, and Chick had decided in what part of the meadows he was.

"I know a big ice house about halfway between Hoboken and Carlstadt," he muttered. "It's out in the marshes, but you can see it from the road. Of course! That's it! I was taken in a boat from the motor car. They rowed me along some of the creeks between the grass swamps, maybe through some of them. Anyhow, I can guess where I am. Now, let me see about getting out."

Chick uttered this last sentence with perfect coolness and confidence. He had no fear of being kept a prisoner for long, especially with his hands and feet free.

That Prince Marcos had been kidnapped at the same time as himself he had no idea.

It had seemed to Chick that his own capture was the logical result of the activity of Nick Carter and himself in helping Marcos to escape the clutches of Solado and Miguel.

The cunning rascals would know that so long as these two clear-sighted, quick-acting detectives were at large, they could not expect to carry out their purpose of holding Prince Marcos away from his own country until they had carried out their treacherous purpose of practically giving it away to another government.

"They're pretty shrewd citizens, I reckon," muttered Chick, as he surveyed his prison. "But they seem to have slipped a cog this time when they left me here without any guard or ropes about me. I'll take the liberty of opening one of those shutters and going out when the time comes."

Chick did not try to do it at once. It was still daylight, and he knew he would have small chance of escape, even if he got out of the building, unless he had some means of leaving the meadows.

"As soon as I am outside, they'll see me, of course," was his reflection. "They could bring me down with a bullet, or they could drop a big stone or chunk of iron on my head, and I'd be all in. I'll have to wait till dark. The only thing against it is that they'll probably have some scheme cooked up before that to put me out."

Chick rubbed his chin musingly. He had had experience enough with the seamy side of humanity to be aware that rascals of the type of Solado and Miguel were not likely to leave a prisoner loosely guarded unless they contemplated a coup to his disadvantage when he should attempt to escape.

It was at this stage of his reflections that he caught the muffled sound of voices. They seemed to come from a corner of his cellar that was a little darker than any other part—if that could be possible.

He stepped softly to the corner and listened. At the same time he detected a dull light close to the wall, which he found came from a place where the stone partition had slightly crumbled away.

The irregular opening thus made was too close to the other wall for him to look through, but it permitted the sound of voices to reach him.

He heard only a few words, but they were illuminating. So Chick pressed his face to the wall, as near as he could get to the hole, to hear more.

All he got as a reward was the sound of a door closing with a bang.

The words that had come to him were in the tones of Miguel, and they were uttered with a savage vindictiveness that made Chick wish he could have been in the adjoining cellar to ram them down the speaker's throat.

"You'll stay here till you give in—or rot!" was what Miguel told the prisoner, whoever he might be.

When the door slammed there was silence, and then it came to Chick that possibly the prisoner might be none other than his beloved chief.

There was no sound reason why it should be Nick Carter who had just been threatened. On the other hand, it might be he, for, if it was considered worth while to take Chick prisoner, was it not probable that Nick had been taken at the same time?

"I'll have to take a chance," muttered Chick. "I must find out who is in that other room."

He squeezed his head into the angle of the wall, in the vain endeavor to bring his eyes level with the opening. Then, in strained accents, he called out:

"Who is in that cellar?"

"Hello!" was the response. "Who is that?"

Chick's sense of hearing was keen, and at once he knew it was Marcos answering him.

"Is it Prince Marcos?" he called out cautiously. "Say 'Yes' if it is. I am a friend of his."

"Yes."

"I thought so. That was Prince Miguel talking to you just now, was it not?"

"Who are you?" was the noncommittal rejoinder. "I don't know you—do I?"

"You ought to. I am Chickering Carter. My boss is Nicholas Carter. We are both trying to help you get back to Joyalita."

"Of course!" replied Marcos heartily. "I beg your pardon for not knowing your voice at first. Have you got a knife?"

"Yes," answered Chick rather wonderingly. "What can I do with that?"

"Use it, when any one comes down to you," was the reply. "They're going to have an interview with you soon, according to what I was just told. You will have to do what they tell you, or—"

There was a pause, and Chick waited for several seconds before he burst out eagerly:

"Well, go on. I have to do as I am told, or—what?"

"You'll have to fight your way out, and I have always thought a knife was the best kind of weapon to use for that purpose," replied Marcos coolly.

CHAPTER VIII

A WATCHFUL ENEMY

"How have they got you?" asked Chick, after a short silence. "Could we not make a break to get out together?"

"If we could get this door down between us, we might," answered Marcos. "It doesn't look so very strong. But I can't find any lock. Are there bolts on your side?"

"No. I can't find anything that feels like a fastening," replied Chick. "Wait a moment! Here's something. I see! The door is nailed shut. There are four or five spikes hammered in around the door. If I had a good stout clawhammer—"

"Sorry I can't help you," came from Marcos, together with the faint odor of a cigarette. "I don't usually carry a clawhammer as part of my equipment. Unfortunately, I haven't anything that might take its place—not even a knife."

The word "knife" gave Chick an idea. He had a jack-knife, in the handle of which were many useful tools. There was no regular nail puller, but one of the implements in the handle was a small pair of highly tempered steel pliers, with serrated edges. They could be used for pulling nails of ordinary size.

The nails holding the door were very large and heavy. Indeed, they were, as Chick had called them, spikes, rather than nails.

"I'll try what I can do," announced Chick, through the hole in the wall. "I've got a pair of pincers that may do the work, because the wood is so rotten. But I'm not sure."

"If I can help at all, by kicking the door, or throwing my weight against it, you can command me," observed Marcos. "We have to get out of this place tonight somehow. I am so confident that your chief, Carter, will do it, if we don't release ourselves, that actually I am not particularly worried."

"You are the real goods," exclaimed Chick admiringly. "I'm going to help you, and I believe we'll make it. If we don't, then you can bet on Nick Carter. Here goes for the spikes!"

It took a long time for Chick to get out the first spike, but he conquered the second one much quicker. He had to use the biggest blade of his knife to cut away the wood around the spikes, as well as the steel pliers. But he persisted, and victory came in each case.

With all his energy, it was two hours before Chick had drawn out the last of the heavy spikes. Then he could not move the door. There were slats of wood nailed in on both sides.

That meant another hour.

He had been encouraged through his work by Marcos, who smoked cigarettes incessantly, and occasionally begged Chick to accept one through the hole in the wall.

But Chick was not much of a smoker at any time. Just now, when he was earnestly at work, he could not be bothered with a cigarette or anything else in the smoking line. So he thanked the prince and declined until both should be outside.

Everything which appeared to hold the door was out of the way at last, and Chick felt that the moment for decisive action had come.

"I'll get a hold on this side with my knife," he told Marcos. "When I say 'Shove!' put all your weight against the door, and I'll pull at the same time. Understand that?"

"Perfectly!" was the prince's drawling reply.

Chick drove the big blade of his knife diagonally into the wood, point downward, until it held firmly. This gave him some power to pull, although not so much as he would have liked.

"I can't help much," he explained. "You'll have to do most of it by your weight. Now! Let her go!"

Chick tugged at the handle of the knife, and, at the same instant, Marcos charged against the door with one of his brawny shoulders. He used all the weight and power he could throw into the effort.

There was a cracking, followed quickly by a smash, and down came the ponderous wooden door to the ground.

Chick jumped out of the way just in time to avoid going down underneath. He had been prepared for the sudden falling of the heavy mass of wood, and had timed his movements exactly.

As the door went down, Marcos walked through the opening and held out his hand to Chick. The two men shook hands gravely.

"Infernally dark in here!" observed Marcos. "But I don't think it is night yet."

"No," returned Chick. "I wish it were. We should have a better chance of getting away. What is your plan? I suppose you have one?"

"Certainly!" answered Marcos, with his customary coolness. "There is a ladder in the far corner of my cellar.

At the top is a trapdoor. I have tried to open it. I can make it crack and strain, but I haven't quite enough strength to push it up altogether."

"The two of us can do it, probably," suggested Chick.

"That's my idea. Once we get through that trap, I don't know what we shall meet. We shall have to take chances on that. I'm going to start for Joyalita tonight."

The calm confidence with which Prince Marcos said this delighted Chick.

Perhaps Chick liked it all the more because the tones of Marcos were so much like Nick Carter's that in the deep gloom he had some difficulty in assuring himself that it was not his chief who was talking.

He could not help referring to it, however.

"You and Mr. Carter are more alike than any two persons I have ever seen in my life," he blurted out. "Even your voices are the same."

"So they tell me," was the careless reply. "But let's get out of this. I've got to get even with that scoundrelly cousin of mine, Miguel, and I'll never do it till I am clear of this bad-smelling place. Come on, Chick!"

"There is a trapdoor in the corner of my cellar, just as there is in yours," remarked Chick. "I guess that is the way they brought me in. But they took away the ladder with them. If they hadn't, we might have gone that way, if this one of yours is too hard a proposition."

Chick lifted the heavy door from the floor, and, with difficulty, extracted the blade of his jackknife.

Marcos was already on the ladder in his own cellar.

Chick found that his companion had rightly estimated the weakness of the trapdoor. When they had both climbed the ladder, so that they could put their hands against it together, they made it yield a little at the very first effort.

"Wait till I cut the wood away around the hinges," suggested Chick. "It's pretty rotten, and it is there that it will give way, if anywhere."

Two minutes sufficed for this work. The knife was very sharp, as well as heavy, and Chick handled it deftly.

"She'll go now!" he declared confidently, as he returned the knife to his pocket. "Now! Together!"

Up went the trap, breaking away from the hinges.

At the same instant, somebody pulled Marcos through the opening and shut the trap down with a bang, knocking Chick off the ladder!

He fell to the ground on his head, and lost consciousness.

When he came to his senses, the cellar was darker than it had been before, and he found himself tightly bound, hand and foot. There was a foul odor coming from somewhere, which seemed to tighten his chest so that he could hardly breathe.

"Ammonia!" gasped Chick, and became senseless again.

CHAPTER IX

AN OFFER OF LIBERTY

When Nick Carter and Patsy began to row toward the back of the warehouse, both were on the alert for any enemy who might be on the watch.

The famous detective knew by experience that the time to expect a hostile surprise was the moment when everything seemed safe, and he was not deceived by the apparent serenity around him.

"Pull into the reeds, Patsy!" he whispered hurriedly.

Patsy obeyed without asking why. He had not seen anything suspicious, but he knew Nick Carter would not give an order without some good reason.

Once in the shelter of the thick, tall grass, however, Patsy looked at his chief for an explanation.

"There's a boat at the back door, Patsy! I can see only the end of the rudder. But that is enough to tell us that if we were around the corner we should come upon the boat itself. You sit still. I'll take the oars."

Patsy yielded the oars without a word.

With extreme caution, Nick Carter pulled through the reeds, without coming out, until he had a clear view of the back door.

Larry Dugan, in the bow of a serviceable skiff—flat-bottomed and solid, like Carter's—was knocking at the heavy door with a blackjack.

Pet Carlin was in the stern, and Foxey Irwin sat amid-ships, oars in his hands.

It was almost dark by this time, and, if the reeds which concealed Nick Carter's boat had not grown almost up to the warehouse, it would have been impossible to make out the door at all.

When Dugan had tapped twice with his lead-weighted, short club, it swung open a little way, and a head protruded.

"Hello, Dugan!"

"Miguel!" muttered Nick Carter. "What's the game, I wonder."

"All right, boss!" was Larry Dugan's response. "We're ready! Let me in!"

"What do you want to come in for?" demanded Miguel. "Your man is ready to pass out."

"That may be. But we've got other business beside taking this guy away," growled Dugan. "There's some stuff of mine in this house that I have to get."

"I'd forgotten that," returned Miguel. "Come in, then."

"I'm coming!" grunted Dugan.

He stepped out of the boat to the stone sill of the door, and, as he disappeared, Foxey Irwin followed.

It was just as Foxey went into the warehouse that another man in the boat, who had been lying along the bottom, as if anxious to keep out of sight, raised himself slightly, so that he could peer over the gunwale.

"That makes four of 'em, chief," remarked Patsy Garvan in a whisper. "Well, I reckon we can get away with them, especially if we get Chick going strong."

"Silence!" was all Nick Carter answered.

He was trying to make out the features of this man. But it was not till the fellow had straightened up and stepped into the doorway, where the light of a lantern showed by this time, that Nick saw he was a pale-faced, slick-haired personage, who seemed to be in mortal terror of personal injury of some kind.

"That fellow looks like a cur," broke out the irrepressible Patsy. "Gee! I'd like to land on him with my left. S'help me! I'd send in a jolt right from my heels."

"Why? Do you know the man?" asked Nick, with a momentary hope that his assistant might be able to give him some information he wanted. "Ever seen him before?"

"Nix! But I don't like his face. His ears aren't set on right, and there's too much bulge each side of his nose. I want to hand him one on general principles, and if you say the word, I'l—"

"Keep quiet!" ordered Nick sternly. "There go the other two, and they have left their boat tied up outside."

Patsy did not speak. But he wondered what was to be the next move.

He did not have long to speculate, for Nick Carter rowed swiftly around the warehouse until he was under the end of the chute by which he had gained entrance before.

"Make the boat fast and come after me, Patsy!"

Patsy deftly hitched the painter rope around the bottom of the chute and knotted it in such a way that there was no fear of its slipping. Then he looked at his chief for further commands.

"Good knot, Patsy!" commended Nick Carter, whose quick eyes took in all details, even when he seemed to be occupied with something else. "Where did you learn it?"

"Went across to Liverpool on an old windjammer when I was a kid. I was too small to go aloft, except in good weather, but you can bet I learned a lot about bending ropes, and I can make 'most any knot that was known in those days."

Patsy said this without anything suggesting bragging. He was merely telling a commonplace truth, as he looked up at Nick Carter to see what he was to do next.

"Come up this chute, after me. Have your gun ready. I mean your pistol; not your duck gun. Keep close to me, but don't do anything till I give the word. And, above all, don't make a noise."

Patsy nodded his comprehension of all this, and crawled up the long chute just behind Nick as softly as a kitten walking across a short-cropped lawn.

With his knife, it took the detective only about half a minute to negotiate the bolted door.

Once in the room where Nick Carter had been before, Nick took out his flash lamp and threw its white glow all about the room.

It was empty, and the heaps of moldy sawdust that he had observed the first time were still undisturbed, showing that nobody had been moving about since he had left the place.

"Ah!" he muttered. "There's the trapdoor in the corner. We'll go down there."

He pointed his flash at the corner, and Patsy understood, even though he had not caught Nick's whispered observations.

Once in the room below, Nick Carter was able to look down the staircase with the broken banister into the office he had been surveying when he had his unfortunate tumble.

"They are not here," he remarked, in a low tone, to Patsy. "There is some other office close by. I feel sure. Come on!"

Once in the office where Nick, from the staircase above, had heard the plotting of Solado and Miguel, he became very busy, searching every corner and looking behind two other desks he found in the room. He wanted to make sure no one else was there.

Nick Carter knew the cunning of Solado as well as the vindictiveness of Miguel, and it would not have surprised him had there been a sudden attack from ambush.

Even if they had killed him, and it had been brought home to them afterward, they could plead self-defense, setting up the argument that even a detective had no right to break into a warehouse that did not belong to him.

Besides, they would say, naturally, that they did not know he was a detective.

"But I'll beat their game, or know the reason why," he muttered.

In one corner of the office was a square wooden partition, which the detective believed concealed the door and staircase to the lower part of the building.

He opened the door of the partition with caution when he found that it was unlocked. He found himself in a small vestibule, which became pitch dark when the door swung back on a spring.

Before turning off his flash—which precautionary measure he had taken ere he let himself into this little lobby—he had seen that there was another door opposite.

Slowly he opened this door. As he did so, a blinding flash of light came in his face. He was looking directly into a lamp with a reflector on the wall of a room adjoining the office from which he had come.

At the same time he was confused by a babel of voices.

It was lucky for Nick Carter that the persons talking were all standing or sitting with their backs toward him— except one.

This one, whose eyes met his own at the moment he thrust part of his head through the opening, was the person he wanted to get into touch with. It was Prince Marcos.

The other three were Solado, Miguel, and the small-eyed, slick-haired individual who had been lying down in the skiff outside the warehouse up to the time he entered.

"I'll give you this last chance, Marcos," Miguel was saying, in harsh, insulting tones. "If you will give me your word of honor to remain in New York for two weeks longer, I will release you at once."

"I wouldn't do it," broke in the slick-haired man. "Keep him where you can be sure of him."

Marcos shot a look of indignant anger at the slick-haired man that made him seem to crumple up, as he said sternly:

"Jason, if ever I get you back in Joyalita, you shall pay for this in a way you deserve. I ought to have taken notice of the warning I had before we left home that you were not to be trusted."

"That's all right!" snarled Jason. "I was as much to be trusted as any one, I suppose. There's Prince Miguel! He's your cousin, and he's going to take your place as head of the country when he gets back. Why don't you talk to him. He's—"

Jason might have said more, for he seemed to be getting more spiteful as he proceeded. But Miguel suddenly jumped from his chair, and, with a stifled oath, sent his fist crashing against Jason's temple.

The rascal fell to the floor without a groan. He did not move afterward.

"Now, Marcos! What do you say?" asked Miguel coolly, as he took his chair again, without even a glance at the prostrate Jason.

"What do I say?" repeated Marcos. "What do I say? Why, I say that you are a more contemptible scoundrel than that poor devil you have just knocked down, and that I shall yet have the pleasure of putting you in the government prison of Joyalita for treason and abduction."

"That's enough!" sneered Miguel. "Go on, Solado!"

Solado rapped with his knuckles on the table before him.

As if he had touched a spring, Larry Dugan, Pet Carlin, and Foxey Irwin dashed into the room from a doorway hidden from Nick Carter by a screen, and pulled Marcos off his feet before he saw that anybody was behind him.

CHAPTER X

CAUGHT ON THE FLY

The three toughs dragged Marcos across the floor and behind the screen so quickly that he was gone before Miguel had time to rise from his chair.

Obviously his intention was to help the three gangsters, but they did not need him, a fact that he recognized even as they disappeared.

"That's the end of that, Solado," remarked Miguel carelessly. "Those fellows will take him to their joint, as they call it, downtown, in New York, and there he will stay till we have completed the treaty in Joyalita—"

"With you as the ruler, under the protection of our allies," added Solado, grinning. "That sounds good. But, if we are going to save trouble immediately, we ought to use the yacht and get him out to sea for a few weeks."

"I don't see that he would be any safer at sea than shut up in some secret den in New York, with these determined-looking gentry we have hired to look after him."

"He would be safer at sea," hissed Solado, "because accidents happen at sea. Yachts sometimes get into trouble on the ocean and are never heard of again."

"You're a cold-blooded rascal, Solado!"

"Not any more than yourself," was the retort. "Only, when I undertake anything, I like to make sure that it is done completely. I have some stake in all this as well as yourself, remember."

"Exactly!" laughed Miguel. "You are still to be at the head of the government—under me, and you want to be sure of your job. Well, I don't blame you. But, for the present, we'll let Dugan take care of my dear Cousin Marcos."

He got up and bent over Jason.

"He won't die!" he decided calmly, as he might have expressed judgment on a half-drowned kitten. "That cuff on the side of his head will be a useful warning to him not to be insolent another time. Come on, Solado! Let's go and see how they get Marcos away."

"Wait a moment!" objected Solado. "They can attend to him, without us. Here are some letters that came for Marcos from Joyalita. We'd better look them over and see what is to be done with them. There is a large part of the population on Marcos' side, you know, and we can't take any chances on rebellion, you know."

Nick Carter remained long enough to see the two plotters put their heads together over a bundle of letters on the table. Then he withdrew, closed the door softly, and rejoined Patsy.

In two minutes more both were at the bottom of the chute, while Patsy untied the boat.

"I'm glad it is dark, Patsy!" whispered Nick Carter. "They are taking Marcos away in that boat, and we have to stop them, if we can. If not, we must trail them till we can get help to take them in."

"We don't need help," snapped Patsy Garvan. "There's only three of them, and if we have this Marcos to help us, there'll be three on our side. Why, I am almost ashamed to do it. It's too easy! Are we to shoot?"

"If we can't nail them any other way. Have you got handcuffs in your pocket, Patsy?"

"Two pairs! I figured we'd need them, even if you have a pair—"

"Which I have," interjected Nick. "I'll row. Get into the bow, with your gun in your hand. As soon as you get where you can make a grab at their boat, cover the nearest man, and I'll do the same with the next. Then make a jump."

"I don't get you," admitted Patsy. "Aren't we liable to tumble into the water?"

"Not if you do your work right. Their boat is tied up to the stone sill of the door. All we have to do is to row up level with it, and I'll get hold of their gunwale. That will hold us steady, and you can throw your gun on your man."

"But you'll be sitting down, and—"

"I can use a gun sitting down, as well as standing up," remarked Nick calmly.

"They are bringing some stuff out of the warehouse," whispered Patsy. "Looks like sacks of coal or something."

"Silver, probably," interrupted Nick. "Look out! They are all in the boat except Dugan. You see that man they have sitting in the stern?"

"Yes. Who is he?"

"Marcos."

"Gee! The king-pin himself! All right! We'll get him so slick, those Jimmy toughs will think they are dancing the tango upside down on a toboggan slide. Just watch me get the drop on that hard-faced guy in the middle."

"That's Foxey Irwin," remarked Nick.

"Don't I know it?" was Patsy's quick rejoinder. "I'm only afraid my bullet may bounce off his face and fly into bits all over this part of the meadows."

Nothing more was said now. Larry Dugan had been piling up sacks of loot in the boat, and Nick Carter doubted not that his pockets were full of jewelry and small articles of value generally.

In the doorway stood Solado and Miguel, and Nick noticed that a small boat, of the same general type as his own and the gangster's, was moored at the other side of the door.

"That boat wasn't there before," observed Patsy, in a whisper.

"They had it inside," returned Nick. "Didn't want to call attention to their presence."

"They're a smooth bunch! Shall we make the rush now?"

"Yes. Be sure to cover your man. That will be Foxey. I'll get Dugan."

"Pet Carlin is the most dangerous!" Patsy reminded him.

"I depend on Marcos getting him," was all Nick said to this.

Like a flash, they shot their boat suddenly out of the tangle of reeds, and so skillfully did Nick Carter guide the craft, that it ran alongside the other as evenly as if there had been the utmost deliberation.

Instantly, excitement broke out in that quiet region, which up till then had been perfectly silent except for the distant quacking of wild ducks who had been skimming the water a mile or so away, the rushing of the evening breeze through the swaying rushes, and the occasional toot of a railroad locomotive taking home a load of commuters.

Patsy swung his revolver over till its muzzle was exactly opposite the right eye of Foxey Irwin, while Nick Carter pointed his automatic steadily at Larry Dugan, with the quiet warning:

"Don't move, Dugan! Half an inch to one side or the other, and I touch the trigger."

"Touch, eh?" sneered Dugan. "Why don't you pull it while you are about it—if you have the nerve to shoot at all."

"A touch is all that is needed with this gun, Dugan," returned Nick. "It's the easiest trigger I ever put my finger on. And I wouldn't advise you to test my nerve about shooting."

Nick Carter would not have parleyed thus if he had not seen that Marcos had sprung at the throat of Pet Carlin and snatched away that innocent-looking person's pistol just as it leaped from his side pocket.

Carlin was known as a "killer," and there is little doubt that he would have tried to "get" Nick Carter at the instant that the detective covered Dugan, if Marcos had not been too quick for him.

Nick had perfect faith in this prince from Joyalita who looked so much like himself. He had seen that Marcos never permitted himself to get rattled, but was always in complete control of his nerves.

So, when Marcos leaped at Carlin just as the other boat swung alongside, anticipating, by a sliver of a second, the drawing of Pet's gun, it was no more than Nick Carter had felt sure would happen.

"Put on the cuffs, Patsy!" whispered Nick to his assistant. "Get Foxey first. Then take Dugan."

"What about the guys in the doorway?" asked Patsy, as he prepared to obey orders.

"I'll look after them. They've got to show me where Chick is."

"That's right! Look out, Foxey!"

This last ejaculation had been caused by a sudden twitch on the part of Foxey Irwin, as Patsy, having stepped from one boat to the other, snapped a handcuff on Foxey's right wrist before he knew what threatened him.

"I'll croak you when I get out of this, Garvan," hissed Foxey.

"Maybe! But that will be in about seven years' time, when you come down from up the river, and there's no telling what may happen before that," replied Patsy, undisturbed.

At the same moment he caught Foxey Irwin's left wrist and trapped it in the other cuff. Patsy had been taught to put on handcuffs long ago, and he could do the work so neatly that it looked like sleight-of-hand to an unaccustomed eye.

Meanwhile, Nick Carter had handcuffed Dugan on his left wrist, holding the other steel bracelet in his own left hand, while his right kept the automatic pointed at Dugan's forehead.

Then it was that the detective worked a little trick on Larry Dugan and Foxey Irwin that he had found useful in dealing with other gentry of their unscrupulous character.

Suddenly pulling Foxey toward him, while giving Dugan a push, he passed the chain of the loose handcuff around the connecting links on Foxey's hands, and instantly snapped the manacle on Dugan's right wrist.

The net result of the maneuver was that the two scoundrels were handcuffed to each other, face to face, and about as helpless as a horse in a balloon.

"Lend me that extra pair of yours, Patsy!" called out Nick.

Patsy gave him the other handcuffs, and they were snapped around Pet Carlin's wrists with disconcerting celerity, while Nick drew the young gunman's second pistol from an outside pocket and placed it in his own.

"Better draw those cuffs tight, chief!" warned Patsy. "Pet has mighty pretty hands. If he was a girl, he'd be wearing a finger ring for a bracelet."

This advice was not called for, however. Nick Carter had taken cognizance of the extreme slimness of Pet Carlin's hand and wrist, and had drawn the steel cuffs so small that they were quite safe.

Hardly had the detective done all this than he made a leap for his own boat again and pulled up to the door.

Solado and Miguel were about to beat a retreat in their private skiff.

"Stop!" shouted Nick Carter.

He accentuated his demand by pointing his own pistol and Pet Carlin's at the heads of the two conspirators.

They stopped.

CHAPTER XI

FROM ONE PERIL TO ANOTHER

"Go into that house again!" commanded Nick. "I want to look through it. And you'll go with me."

"What for?"

"You know what for," thundered Nick. "You have my assistant in there, Chickering Carter. I'm going to get him out. Come on!" he continued, more fiercely than ever, as he waved his pistol. "Any hesitation, and I swear I will shoot the pair of you. I ought to do so, anyhow, for your treason to Prince Marcos."

"What have you to do with Prince Marcos?" snarled Miguel. "The politics of Joyalita are no concern of yours."

"Breaking the law in New York or New Jersey is very much a concern of mine. I have enough against you now to hold you. If any harm comes to my man, you will be responsible."

He had jumped out of his boat to the stone sill of the door into the warehouse, and was close to the two rascals.

"Go in first, and I will follow!"

He prodded his gun against the chest of Miguel, and there was a look in the detective's eye that would have told any one it was dangerous to play with him. But Miguel did not give way.

"I'm not going in there again," he growled.

"Yes, you will. I—"

Nick Carter stopped. He had caught the steady thump of an engine, and he remembered that he had heard the sound himself when a prisoner in the cellar.

It had stopped when he made his escape. But it had been set going again.

The detective did not hesitate any longer. He pushed Miguel ahead of him, at the same time pointing one of his pistols at Don Solado.

"Show me the place! Show it to me, quick!" he shouted. "I know it is the cellar. But how do you get down to it? Quick!"

Only the knowledge that Chick was in deadly peril within a few yards of him, and that if he took the time to find out for himself how to reach his prison, it might be too late, prevented Nick Carter from shooting Miguel dead on the spot.

"I'll show you!" volunteered Solado.

"Fool!" mumbled Miguel, in too low a tone for Nick Carter to hear.

"Where is the door?" demanded Nick.

"Here! In this corner, behind these barrels!" answered Solado. "Here is the key. It is barred outside, too."

Nick began to tear away the barrels, taking no notice of Solado or Miguel. He had something more important to engage his attention just then.

The deadly fumes of ammonia were coming from the chinks of the cellar, and, as he turned the key, kicked away the bar, and pulled the door open, they came pouring out in a volume that staggered him for a moment.

"Chick!" he called.

There was no answer.

Nick Carter turned the powerful gleam of his flash light into the gloomy depths, and a low cry of horror broke from him.

Lying on the floor, against the wall, his limbs contorted and his face buried in his arms, as if he had resisted the deadly gas as long as he could, was Chick.

It was not necessary for Nick Carter to see the face to know who it was. He would have recognized the general appearance of his beloved first assistant even if he had not known him by his clothes.

"Chick!" he repeated, in an agonized groan, as he pressed a handkerchief over his nose and mouth. "Chick! Keep your mouth covered!"

"Chief!"

The response came in a far-away gasp, as if it were almost the last effort the speaker was capable of making.

It was enough for Nick Carter.

Indeed, he had not waited for a reply. Even while he spoke to Chick he had begun to descend the steep ladder in the corner of the cellar.

With a bound he crossed the floor and picked up his assistant in his arms.

"Keep your mouth covered!" mumbled Nick Carter, through his handkerchief.

It was instinct that made Chick press his two hands over his mouth.

Nick crawled along, keeping as low as he could to avoid at least some of the strength of the poisonous ammonia.

The engine thudded unseen in another compartment of the big cellar, pumping more of the gas from the generator to the storage tank, whence some demoniac villainy had arranged for it to escape.

"This will be all for Solado and Miguel," thought Nick, as he half carried, half dragged, Chick across the floor.

He had reached the bottom of the ladder, when a loud, derisive laugh overhead came to his ears. Then, with a bang, the door closed!

Instantly Nick dropped at full length, taking Chick with him.

He wanted a moment to think, and it was essential that he should inhale as little of the ammonia as possible while he decided what to do.

The situation was a terrifying one. To a man less courageous than Nick Carter, it might have appeared hopeless.

"The window!" he muttered. "I know how I got out of the other cellar, by Patsy helping me from the outside. This time I'll have to get it open by my own efforts."

He drew from his pocket the heavy jackknife without which he never went out. Included in its tools was a miniature brace and bit. He fitted this for use as he crawled toward the window.

With his handkerchief tied over his mouth and nose, to keep out as much of the gas he could, Nick got his brace and bit ready for action and pulled himself to his feet.

A few seconds of work bored a hole through the wood. It was old and rotten, and the bit was keen and highly tempered.

The hole was by the side of a nail, whose point Nick had discerned coming through the wood.

"Two more holes, at the other nails, and we'll be through," he muttered. "If only I can hold out so long!"

It was a narrow squeak. But when a man is fighting for his life, he'll keep on against odds, no matter what sort of contest he may have on his hands.

Just as Nick felt that he could not bear the awful pressure of the gas on his lungs another instant, he pushed the boards out of the opening.

As the ammonia poured out, a rush of fresh air came in.

The detective drew it into his system with a joyful gratitude, such as he had seldom felt in all his adventurous life.

Only for a second did he stand there, however. Chick was lying on the floor, and though, in that position, he had not been affected so strongly by the poison as he would have been if standing up straight, it had rendered him entirely unconscious.

Taking up his assistant in his strong arms, Nick lifted him so that his head rested on the stone ledge, where he got the full benefit of the cool night air from the salty waters.

"This is all right so far as it goes!" muttered the detective. "But I don't want to swim. I'd have to hold Chick up in the water, too. He is all in for the present."

He stared out into the gloom, but nothing could he make out except the dim sky line of the rushes and the banks of heavy clouds which obscured the stars over in the east.

It was a desolate scene.

So far as he could discern, there were no boats in the neighborhood, and for a moment he heard no sound of voices.

Then he caught the sharp accents of Patsy, commanding Pet Carlin to keep still. This was followed by a growling oath that might have been the utterance either of Larry Dugan or Foxey Irwin.

"Patsy has all he can attend to," decided Nick. "He's waiting for me to come out. I'll have to bring him around to this side. There is nothing else for it, although some of those blackguards are liable to jump him if he settles down to row."

Nick actually had his mouth open to call to his wide-awake second assistant, when a crash that might have meant the blowing up of the whole building stopped him.

The sound began with a swish such as often precedes the boom of an explosion of certain kinds of chemicals.

It was followed immediately by a heaven-splitting cr-r-rack, and then by the thunderous letting go of what might have been one of the heaviest guns known to modern ordnance.

Simultaneously, the big wooden warehouse rocked on its foundations, and Chick fell from the window ledge back to the cellar.

Down went Nick to the floor after him. He had only just got there, and placed his hands on the clothing of his assistant, when another explosion, even more terrifying than the first, sent the stone-wall foundations scattering in all directions.

Nick found himself hemmed in by heaps of splintered wood, while the upper part of the building, caving in one side, formed an arch over him that threatened to collapse at any moment.

"Chick!" he cried. "Where are you?"

There was no answer. He had not expected any.

His assistant had slipped from his grasp at the second explosion, and the general disturbance had separated them. In the heaps of débris it was impossible for Nick to see him at once.

"Heaven preserve us!" muttered the detective. "I've *got* to find him!"

Outside the building he could hear Patsy shouting to him, while the oaths of the prisoners, as they commanded Patsy to get the boat farther away from the destroyed warehouse, told plainly enough that his second assistant had special troubles of his own.

"Patsy!" cried Nick, at the top of his voice. "Stay where you are! I'll bring Chick!"

He did not know whether his voice had carried to Patsy or not. Indeed, he had no time to think about it, for suddenly, with a vicious roar, a blue-and-yellow tongue of flame shot up from the middle of the great heaps of timbers about him, and through the caved-in roof overhead.

The warehouse was on fire!

CHAPTER XII

ROUNDED UP

"Chick!" shouted Nick Carter, in agony. "Where are you?"

Again there was no answer. Nick Carter would have been surprised if there had been. Well he knew that if Chick was to be rescued, it must be without any help from the imperiled one himself.

Fragments of blazing timbers were beginning to fall, and Nick saw that if certain joists already on fire should burn through, down would come the tons of flooring and roof upon his head. Nothing could save him.

If he meant to get Chick out of this, he must do it quickly.

"There he is—on the other side of that heap of burning wood," he muttered. "Merciful heavens! Some of it is resting on him. He may be slowly roasting to death! I must get to him!"

It was a perilous trip the detective had now.

Mounds of rubbish had been built up by the explosions, and had caught fire afterward. Nick had to climb over them.

That the fire was incendiary there could be no doubt. Indeed, Nick Carter had heard enough of the plots of the two rascals from Joyalita, as well as of the Dugan gang, to know that the whole affair had been planned.

The only place where the plot had fallen down from the original intention was in the escape of Marcos.

He was to have been burned to death in this warehouse, and the explosions, arranged so that they should end in a general conflagration, were prepared for his destruction.

The fact that Chick was in the building, too, was merely an incident. It is not likely that the explosions would have been caused just for him alone. Still, as he chanced to be in the way of them, why, so much the better, in the opinion of the conspirators.

Dugan and his gang had been seeking to get Nick Carter and his principal assistant out of the way for years.

Nick was not bothering about that now. He had just climbed to the top of a blazing pile, and found Chick lying in a hollow on the other side.

Suddenly the heated mass gave way beneath him!

"I don't care!" gasped Nick Carter, as he drew one foot out of a hole, where it seemed as if the leather of his shoe must be burned through. "I've got to get him out of this! I'd do it or—go with him!"

This was no idle talk. He meant it.

It will be remembered that Nick wore a pair of high wading boots, which were of leather below and up to his knees, with rubber above, covering his thighs.

There is little doubt that these stout, high boots did a large part in enabling him to reach Chick. They protected him to some extent, where low shoes and trousers would surely have meant painful, if not fatal, burns.

He plowed through the awful smoking mass till he found himself standing right over his unconscious assistant.

"Now, Chick! If only you were a little like yourself, how easy it would be!" muttered Nick. "But there is no use in wishing. I've got to take him the best way I can."

Stooping over and getting a firm hold, he lifted the young man and swung him over one shoulder. Then, without stopping to look one way or the other, he began his journey back to the window.

It took him five minutes to accomplish this feat, and more than once, when a quantity of burning rubbish came tumbling about his ears, he believed it was all up with him and his helpless burden.

But in some almost miraculous way he got through, and resting Chick on the stone coping at the window opening, looked around for a means of escape.

"Chief!" shouted Patsy, from his boat among the rushes. "Wait a moment! I'll be there!"

"That's what you won't!" roared Larry Dugan, in impotent wrath. "You ain't going to run me into no such risks as that. If you want to put me in jail, all right. But—"

A large, open hand came rattling across the side of Dugan's face and shut off his eloquence. The owner of the hand—none other than Prince Marcos—called out to Patsy to drive the boat close to the window.

"We shan't be burned," he added. "Anyhow, we have to take that risk. We can't leave those two men there. Mr. Carter can swim, I know. But Chick is done for, unless somebody helps him."

"Hello! Here's luck!" suddenly exclaimed Patsy. "Gee! This is my good night!"

The skiff in which he and Nick Carter had come to the ice house was floating about near him. A few quick pulls on the oars, and he was able to reach the empty boat.

"Here is my gun," he said simply, to Marcos, as he handed him his revolver. "If Larry Dugan or either of the others gets at all gay, just put a lead pill into his coco. All you have to do is to get the end of the barrel against the patient's ear. Then pull this little dingus underneath, and it will cure the nervousness right away."

Marcos laughed at Patsy's prescription for the prisoners as he took the revolver.

"You hear what the doctor says, gentlemen!" he remarked, bringing the muzzle of the pistol to bear on Larry Dugan's sinister countenance. "Don't jump about too much, or I might pull the—er—dingus by accident."

Patsy was up to the window where Nick Carter supported Chick in a very few seconds.

"Gee, chief! This joint looks as if it was going to fold in on itself any minute. Listen to the fire spitting. And talk about a smell! They must have forgot to clean off the kindling wood before they started this one. In with him! All right, Chick! Don't worry! It's your Uncle Patsy has you now! Say! This is a hot one, all right!"

Chatting in this way to keep up his own spirits, as well as to make Chick feel safe in case he should be coming to his senses, Patsy Garvan helped Nick Carter lift Chick into the boat.

"Pull, Patsy! Pull for your life!" shouted Nick, as Patsy got the pair of oars well in hand.

"Sure I'll pull!" was the hearty response. "I can tumble without a house falling on me!"

Nick Carter could not aid his willing assistant at that instant. There was only one pair of oars in the skiff, and Patsy had them.

"Hello! Those walls are going to fall out!"

Instinctively, Nick tried to shield Chick, lying in the bottom of the boat, by bending over him, as part of the blazing ruins broke down again.

A flying board, all blue flames and scattering sparks, came charging full tilt at the boat.

It struck Nick Carter's arm, and fell, seething, into the water. If it had come straight in its original course, it must have plunged into the unprotected, upturned face of Chick.

"That was a close call," observed Patsy, as he ran the skiff up against the other one, where Marcos was keeping close watch on the prisoners. "What shall I do now?"

"Get in and row the gang to shore. I'll take Chick in this skiff. He is beginning to come around," returned Nick.

"Sure!" almost screamed Patsy, in an excess of delight.

"Hello, Patsy!" said Chick feebly.

"Gee! That's a good sound!" ejaculated Patsy. "All right, chief! I'll be responsible for these three beauties. Now that I know Chick is all to the good, I could handle two gangs of this size. Trust me!"

Nick hurriedly rowed to the place where he had hired the boat, and, in the comfortable home of the man who owned the place, soon had Chick on his feet again—shaky, but otherwise all right.

"I'll leave you here tonight, if you like, Chick," said Nick, after a short conference with the boat owner. "He says he can take care of you until morning. We have to ride on the street car, you know. There won't be one along for an hour, anyhow."

"By that time I'll be fit as a fiddle," declared Chick. "Let me go with you."

"Say, chief!" asked Patsy, who was standing guard over the three disgruntled gangsters, in company with Marcos. "What became of those two other guys from Joyalita?"

"I can tell you that," put in Marcos gravely. "They have got away. They had a motor car here, and when we were occupied in looking after Dugan and his men, and trying to help Mr. Carter find Chick in that warehouse, they took advantage of nobody watching them. That is all. So long as they cannot prevent my reaching Joyalita, I am not particular about going after them. The man Jason must have died in the fire."

"You shall start for Joyalita in the morning, if you like," smiled Nick Carter. "It looks as if we have beaten the whole plot against you."

"Thanks to you, Mr. Carter!"

Prince Marcos held out his hand to the detective, while Dugan, still handcuffed to Foxey Irwin, snorted in angry disgust.

"By the way, I have your watch, the Seal of Gijon," said Nick. "I have never had an opportunity to give it to you till now."

He brought out the precious diamond-incrusted watch and jeweled fob which had been the subject of his close inspection, and about whose secret spring he was still puzzled, and handed it to Marcos.

As the prince took the watch, he pressed it to his lips. Then he put it to his forehead, with a gesture of reverence. At the same time he murmured a few words in a strange tongue, that Nick Carter did not understand.

Even when Marcos had hidden the watch in an inner pocket of his waistcoat, he did not speak for a minute, at least.

It seemed as if there were a sacred significance attached to the Seal of Gijon which made it sacrilege to talk on outside matters for a short period after handling the precious emblem.

It was more than an hour before a street car came bowling along the lonely road which ran through the meadows, and which might have been a thousand miles from a city, judging by its desolate appearance, instead of only a few miles from the metropolis itself.

The conductor was a stolid individual, and when he saw that there were three handcuffed men pushed into the car ahead of four other men—for Chick had recovered sufficiently to go along with his friends—he only wondered what the trio had been pinched for, and let it go at that.

There were three heavy sacks lifted upon the back platform, and Patsy stood out there with them, his hand close to the butt of a revolver in his coat pocket.

All the notice the conductor took of this was to grumble, sotto voce, as conductors often do, in similar cases:

"Why don't youse guys hire an express wagon?"

If the conductor had known that in those sacks was stolen property aggregating in value not less than two hundred thousand dollars, he might have shown a little more interest.

It was early in the morning when Nick Carter turned over to the officers at police headquarters his three prisoners, Larry Dugan, Foxey Irwin, and Pet Carlin. He also handed in, and got a receipt for, the three bags of loot that he had captured with the Dugan gang.

Then he went home, with Chick and Patsy, to enjoy a good breakfast, while Marcos, in a taxicab, hurried back to Crownledge, to relieve the mind of his pretty cousin, Claudia Solado, and complete his preparations to return at once to Joyalita.

"And you owe it all to Mr. Carter," remarked Claudia, as she presided at the breakfast table, with Phillips in attendance.

"Indeed I do," declared Marcos enthusiastically. "If he would come to Joyalita, I would make him prime minister."

The young girl laughed. She shook her head and said:

"I am afraid there is no office in Joyalita important enough to lure Nick Carter away from New York."

"No, I suppose not," returned Marcos slowly. "But what a fine head of the government he'd make. I'd like to see him dealing with a bunch of conspirators like these of my Cousin Miguel's."

"I believe he'd take them up in his two strong hands and bang their heads together," opined Claudia, with another merry laugh.